NOV. 7

CHADRON (NE) STATE COLLEGE

5086 00389983 6

W9-BUR-626

ERIN'S VOYAGE

WRITTEN BY JOHN FRANK
ILLUSTRATED BY DENA SCHUTZER

SIMON & SCHUSTER BOOKS FOR YOUNG READERS
Published by Simon & Schuster
New York London Toronto Sydney Tokyo Singapore

SIMON & SCHUSTER BOOKS FOR YOUNG READERS
1230 Avenue of the Americas
New York, New York 10020
Text copyright © 1994 by John Frank
Illustrations copyright © 1994 by Dena Schutzer
All rights reserved including the right of
reproduction in whole or in part in any form.
SIMON & SCHUSTER BOOKS FOR YOUNG READERS
is a trademark of Simon & Schuster.
The text for this book is set in 14-point Schneidler Medium.
The illustrations were done in oils.
Manufactured in the United States of America

10 9 8 7 6 5 4 3 2 1

Library of Congress Cataloging-in-Publication Data
Frank, John.   Erin's voyage / by John Frank ;
illustrated by Dena Schutzer.   p.   cm.
Summary: Erin discovers a doll that has been in her grandfather's
attic for many years and makes a nighttime voyage to return the doll
to her rightful owner.
[1. Dolls—Fiction.   2. Seashore—Fiction.]   I. Schutzer,
Dena, ill.   II. Title.
PZ7.F8512Er   1994   [E]—dc20   92-31783   CIP   AC
ISBN 0-671-79585-6

+
E
F851e

For my mother and father
—J.F.

For Marian Reiner
—D.S.

Every summer Erin visited her grandfather at his country house. Her favorite room was the attic. In the afternoons she'd sit in the old stuffed chair by the window facing the western sky. And she'd wait, as the sun passed over the pond, for the restless light on the distant sea.

One day as Erin pushed open the attic door, a box perched on the edge of a high shelf fell to the floor. It was made of dark wood, and had brass hinges and a silver clasp.

Erin picked up the box and blew off the dust. She rubbed her sleeve over the wood until she could see her reflection, tangled in a web of tiny cracks. Then she unhooked the silver clasp and lifted back the lid.

Inside, cushioned on a bed of straw, was a doll unlike any she'd ever seen.

Erin hurried downstairs to show her grandfather.
Grandpa rubbed his chin thoughtfully. "When your
great-great-grandmother Clara was your age," he said,
"she found this doll at the seashore, wedged among
the rocks."

"How did it get there, Grandpa?" asked Erin.

"Probably brought by the waves. People
thought the doll came from a ship lost at
sea. Even so, Clara felt she should try to
find its owner. She posted signs asking
the owner to come claim it, but no
one ever did."

Erin studied the doll's bright eyes and touched its faded bonnet.

"She's been locked in that box an awfully long time," Grandpa said. "If I give her to you, will you try to make her feel at home?"

"Oh yes, Grandpa!" Erin lifted the doll out of the box and carefully brushed away the straw. For the rest of the day, she took the doll with her wherever she went.

And at bedtime she laid its head on a
pillow next to her own.

Late that night Erin was wakened by the sound of the wind. She slid out from under the covers, picked up the doll, and silently went up to the attic. As she looked out toward the pond, the mast of a sailboat appeared among the reeds, framed in the circle of the moon.

Erin turned and followed the stairs
back down to her bedroom. Quietly, she
dressed herself. With the doll in her arms,
she hurried down the hallway, unlatched
the front door, and slipped out into
the moonlight.

She hiked across the field of grass, and then wove
her way through a thick cluster of reeds. Finally, she
came to a clearing. There was the sailboat, floating in
the shallows of the pond.

For a moment the wind paused to gather its breath.
And at that same moment, there came a faint cry, a
distant voice that seemed to call Erin's name.

Erin laid the doll on the seat of the boat and climbed in. She raised the sail, and then swung it around to catch the wind.

The boat glided away from the bank. Guiding the sail with her left hand and the rudder with her right, Erin crossed over to where the pond narrowed into a creek. When she felt the tug of the flowing water, she lowered the sail.

The current began to gather speed, braiding the water into swirling strands. Suddenly, the boat was swept into a rushing river. Erin clutched the doll to her chest as the boat pitched its way downstream.

Before long the river turned silent and slow, losing its boldness as it neared the sea. As the air grew sharp with the scent of brine, Erin again raised the sail. The wind grabbed hold and the boat bobbed ahead over the moonlit tide.

Once again came the cry of the faraway voice, but the tiny sound was swallowed by the wind and the waves, and Erin could not be sure the name was her own.

Up ahead, through the mist, a wooden ship appeared, rocking slowly in the water, its bare masts ignoring the wind. Standing at the bow, clasping the railing, was a small girl.

Erin lowered her sail, then fitted an oar to each side of her boat. She rowed up to the ship's long hull and tied fast to a rope ladder that hung from the deck.

With the doll under one arm, Erin struggled up the ladder and hoisted herself on board. The girl was waiting.

She and Erin stood facing each other, the
timbers beneath them creaking with the sway
of the ship. Slowly, Erin held out the doll.

The girl cradled the doll in her arms. "My sweet
Ann," she said softly. "I've been calling you for the
longest time."

A low whistle of wind blew across the deck. Erin
reached out and touched the doll for the last time.
"I'll miss her," Erin said to the girl. "But now I know
she's home."

Lowering herself into the boat and freeing the rope, Erin set off again, riding the waves back toward the river.

When Erin reached the mouth of the river, the
wind was gusting hard. Fighting against the current, it
pushed the boat upstream. Even after the boat came
to the creek, the wind wouldn't rest. Only when Erin
had reached the bank of the pond and was headed
back across the field to her grandfather's house did
the wind begin to die down.

At the front door, Erin pulled off her boots and
slipped inside. Back in her bedroom, she changed into
her nightgown and crawled under the covers.

Erin's grandfather came into the room and sat down on the edge of the bed.

"I've been to the ship, Grandpa," Erin said. "The doll's name is Ann."

"*Ssshhh,*" said Grandpa, stroking Erin's cheek. "The wind has been giving you strange dreams. Try to go back to sleep." Erin closed her eyes, and her grandfather leaned over and kissed her on the head.

As her grandfather sat up, a puzzled look crossed his face.

Erin's hair, he thought. It smells of the sea.